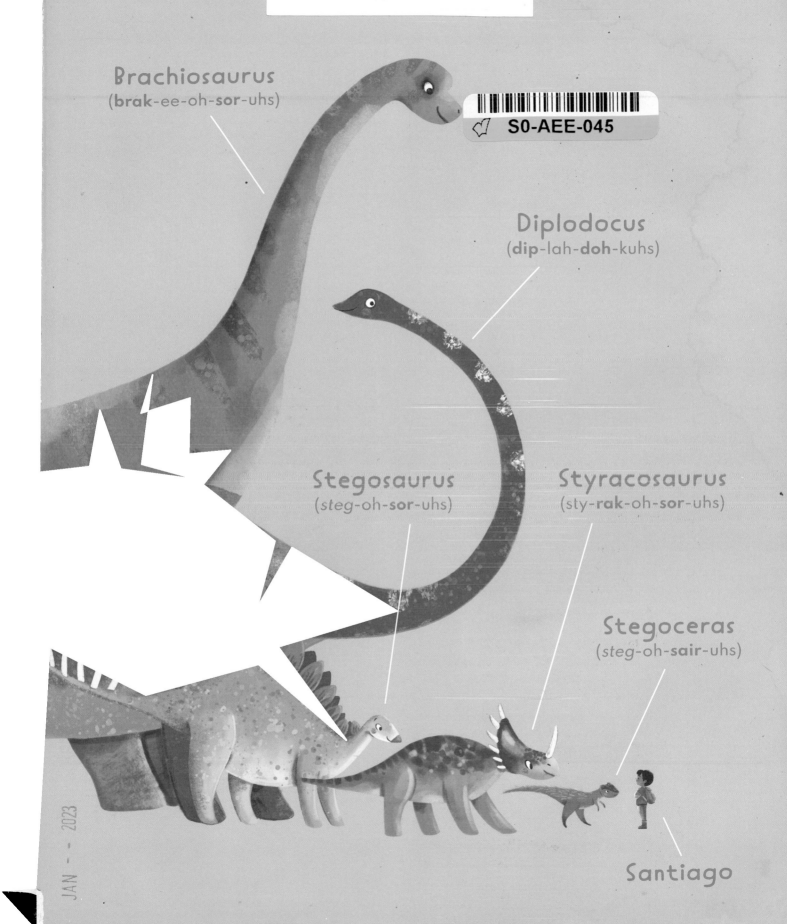

SANTIAGO'S DINOSAURIOS

HELLO!

¡HOLA!

DINOSAURIOS

Mariana Ríos Ramírez

illustrated by Udayana Lugo

ALBERT WHITMAN & COMPANY
CHICAGO, ILLINOIS

Santiago's heart beats fast
as he prepares his backpack.
He includes his lucky *Ankylosaurus* pencil,
his *Tyrannosaurus rex* sharpener,
and his favorite dinosaur book.

But Santiago is still not ready...

to be the new boy,
in a new school,
in a new town,
in a new country...

AND he doesn't understand English.

¿Cómo haré nuevos amigos? *
he wonders on his way to school.

*How will I make new friends?

Santiago peeks inside
Mrs. Taylor's first grade classroom.
He hears the excited chattering
of his new classmates,
but he can't understand them.

"Quiero irme a mi casa,"* he mumbles with teary eyes.

*"I want to go home."

"Class, this is Santiago," Mrs. Taylor says. "His family just moved here from Mexico."

Santiago feels like a dinosaur fossil in a museum as fifteen kids stare at him.

"Hey! Sit here!" A boy waves
and then points down to an
empty chair beside him.

Like a *T. rex* rushing after its prey,
Santiago hurries to sit down.

"Me llamo Santiago."*

"I'm Riley. Welcome to our class!"

Santiago doesn't understand
or know what else to say.

He has a *Brachiosaurus*-sized
problem.

*"My name is
Santiago."

During library time, Santiago enjoys the pictures in a book about the Jurassic period.

"That dinosaur's huge!" Isaac whispers.

"Es un *Diplodocus*," Santiago mumbles. "Tiene cuello largo y come plantas."*

*"It's a *Diplodocus*. It has a long neck and eats plants."

Isaac shrugs. "I...don't understand. I love trains,"
he says. "You know? Choo choo?"

Santiago understands "choo choo" but nothing else.
Isaac turns back to his book.

Santiago has a *Diplodocus*-sized problem.

Music class is no fun for Santiago.
He can't sing along and feels lost in his silence.

¿Será siempre así de aburrido? he wonders.

*Will it always be this boring?

"Psst! Psst!" a voice whispers.
"Your T-shirt is SO cool!"

Actually, Santiago's problem
might only be *Iguanodon*-sized.

After music class, Santiago meets Mrs. Brooks,
and she takes him to her classroom.

"¡Bienvenido, Santiago!"* she says.
"You and I will work together here."

*"Welcome, Santiago!"

"Don't worry! You'll learn English soon," she adds.

Santiago doesn't understand everything
Mrs. Brooks says, but she seems nice, and he
can tell she wants to help him. He takes a deep
breath and gets ready to learn new words.

Now Santiago's problem seems
to be *Parasaurolophus*-sized.

Later, in art class, Santiago creates a *Triceratops* masterpiece.

"That's amazing!" Georgia says. "Look at my cat! Isn't it cute?"

"¡Gato!" Santiago says. "Cat!"

"Yes! Blue cat," she says. "Blue gato."

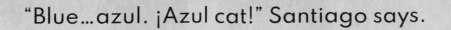

"Blue…azul. ¡Azul cat!" Santiago says.

Both kids chuckle. "¡Azul gato!"

Santiago's problem has become
Stegosaurus-sized.

In the cafeteria, Santiago sits next to Aniya.
He's pleased to find dinosaur nuggets in his lunchbox.

"Your nuggets look yummy! Lucky you!
I have tuna salad again," she says.

Santiago stares at Aniya's lunch;
he's not a tuna fan either.

"¿Quieres?"* Santiago asks.

*"Want some?"

"Into the lava you go!" She giggles.

"Lava!" Santiago repeats,
and both kids laugh.

Santiago feels hopeful about his
Styracosaurus-sized problem.

During recess, Santiago watches
from a distance as his classmates play.

*¿Realmente podré comunicarme pronto?** he wonders.

Suddenly...

*Will I really be able to communicate soon?

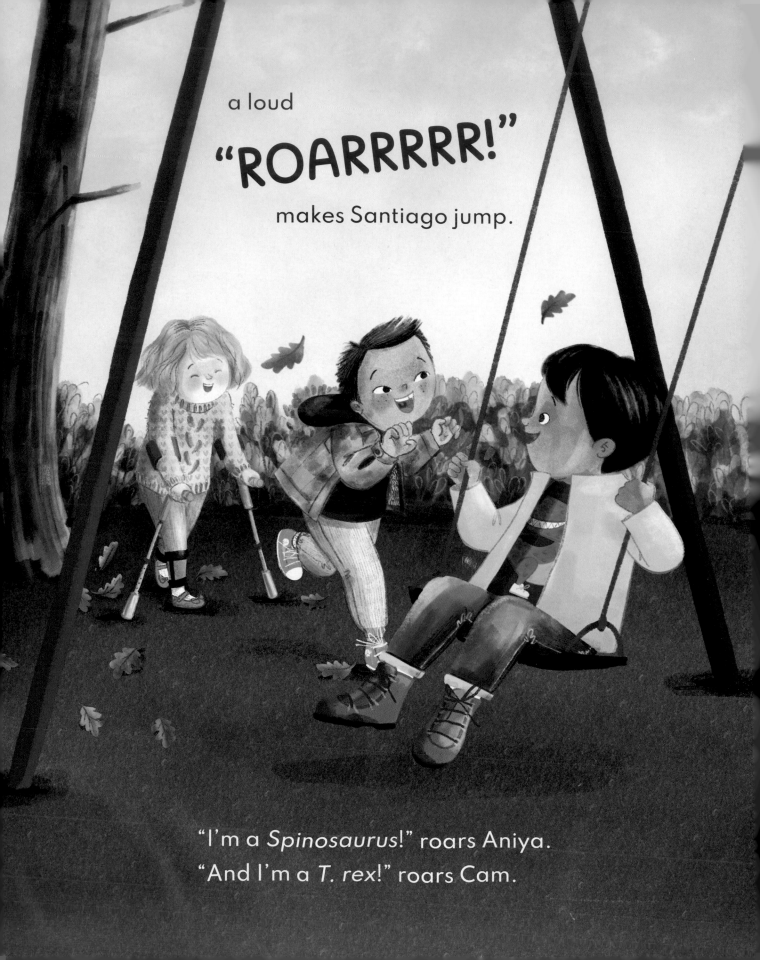

a loud

"ROARRRRR!"

makes Santiago jump.

"I'm a *Spinosaurus*!" roars Aniya.
"And I'm a *T. rex*!" roars Cam.

Santiago holds his breath.
The kids speak dinosaur;
THAT he understands!

Santiago roars "*Velociraptor!*"
and chases after them.

By the end of the day, Santiago's eyes sparkle. As he waits for his mom, he shares his dinosaur book with Aniya and Cam. The children roar and giggle as they turn the pages.

Santiago's dinosaur-sized problem
now resembles a *Stegoceras*.

And although it's not extinct yet,
Santiago knows that one day it will be.

When his mom arrives,
Santiago waves.
"¡Adiós, friends!"

"Bye, amigo!"
Cam and Aniya reply.

This time Santiago
understands and knows
exactly what to say.

So he turns back
and gives his friends
one
last
ROAR.

Glosario de dinosaurios*

Dinosaurios que comen carne (Dinosaurs that eat meat)

Spinosaurus

Espinosaurio

Tyrannosaurus rex

Tiranosaurio rex

Velociraptor

Velociraptor

*Dinosaur glossary

Dinosaurios que comen plantas (Dinosaurs that eat plants)

Ankylosaurus

Anquilosaurio

Brachiosaurus
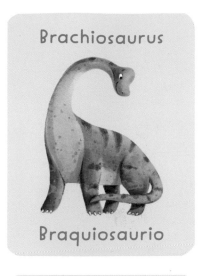
Braquiosaurio

Diplodocus

Diplodocus

Stegosaurus

Estegosaurio

Styracosaurus
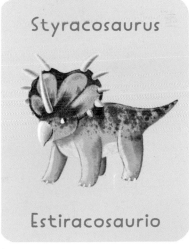
Estiracosaurio

Iguanodon

Iguanodonte

Parasaurolophus

Parasaurolophus

Stegoceras

Stegoceras

Triceratops

Triceratops

For Pato, Lara, and all the brave children around the world
who find new homes in foreign lands—MRR

For all the people who have to make a home, a family,
and friends in a new country—UL

Library of Congress Cataloging-in-Publication data is on file with the publisher.
Text copyright © 2022 by Mariana Ríos Ramírez
Illustrations copyright © 2022 by Albert Whitman & Company
Illustrations by Udayana Lugo
First published in the United States of America in 2022 by Albert Whitman & Company
ISBN 978-0-8075-7230-6 (hardcover)
ISBN 978-0-8075-7232-0 (ebook)
Printed in China
10 9 8 7 6 5 4 3 2 1 WKT 26 25 24 23 22

Design by Aphelandra

For more information about Albert Whitman & Company,
visit our website at www.albertwhitman.com.

Los problemas tamaño dinosaurio de Santiago*

Iguanodon
(ig-oo-**wah**-nah-dahn)

Parasaurolophus
(**pair**-uh-*sor*-uh-**loh**-fus)

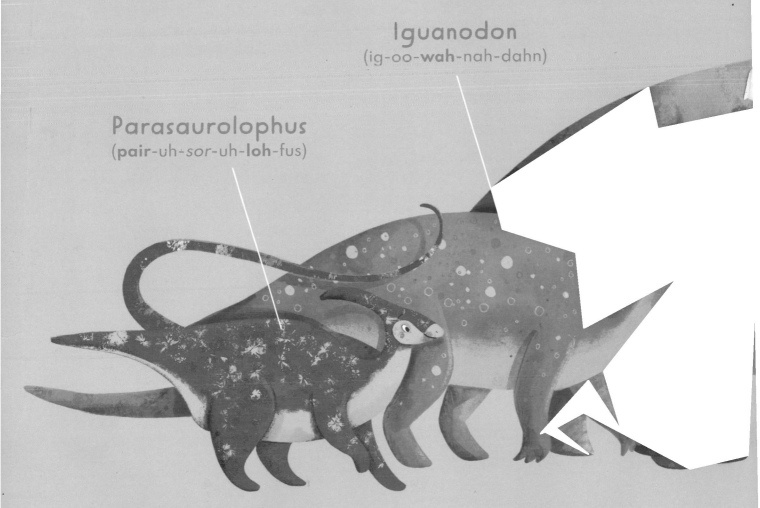

*Santiago's dinosaur-sized problems